Buckley
and
Wilberta
Forever Friends

Hope Slaughter
by **Hope Slaughter**

illustrated by **Susan Torrence**

RED HEN PRESS

*For friend and "editor"
Lee,
with many thanks for
lending her skill
and patience.
H.S.*

To Erin & Evan Truck—
"forever
friends"

Text © 1998 by Hope Slaughter   Illustrations © 1998 by Susan Torrence

RED HEN PRESS
P.O. Box 454
Big Sur, CA 93920

Library of Congress Cataloging in Publication Data
Slaughter, Hope, 1940-Buckley and Wilberta forever friends / by Hope Slaughter ;
illustrated by Susan Torrence.   p .   cm .
Summary : Buckley the hedgehog and Wilberta the rabbit have their friendship tested being snowbound,
making a snowrabbit, overcoming fear of thunder, and surviving a spring flood.
ISBN 0-931093-16-3 (hardcover)
[1. Hedgehogs—Fiction. 2. Rabbits—Fiction. 3. Friendship—Fiction.] I. Torrence, Susan, ill. II. Title.
PZ7.S63115Bw 1998   [E]—DC21   97-40844 CIP AC
Printed in the United States of America

CONTENTS

SNOWBOUND

Buckley watched lazy snowflakes
drift past the window.
"Look at all that snow,"
he said to Wilberta.
Wilberta sighed.
She got so lonely
when she stayed
by herself in winter.
She was spending the winter
at Buckley's house.
"It's been snowing
for days and days," she said.

"I think I'll practice rolling
 this morning," Buckley said.
Wilberta sighed again.
"I guess I could bake
a carrot-nut cake," she said.
She went to the kitchen.
Buckley kneeled down
on his exercise mat.
"Hup, hup, huuuuup," he grunted,
"and over!"
He tucked in his feet
and rolled into a spiney ball.

"Do you have to shout *hup, hup?*"
Wilberta called.

"Oh, sorry," Buckley answered.

"It helps me to roll.
I'll do my push-ups instead.

"One, two, three, *up*.
One, two, three, *down*.
One, two, three, *up* . . . "

"Buckley," Wilberta called,
"must you count *every* push up?"

"Oh, sorry," Buckley said.
He whispered. *"One, two, three, up.
One, two, three, down."*

"All this exercise
makes me hungry," Buckley said.
"I think I'll eat a few nuts."
He took a bowl of chestnuts
from the cupboard.
He sat down by the fire.
"Crack, scrish, smack, ummmm..."
"Do you have to make
so much noise
when you eat nuts, Buckley?"
Wilberta said.
"And you're getting nutshells
all over the rug."
Buckley pushed the bowl aside.
"I've eaten enough nuts
anyway," he said.
"Ummm, your cake smells wonderful."
"You can't cut a piece
until it's cooled," Wilberta said.

Buckley stared at the fire.

"I can't do anything right," he said.

"Oh, Buckley," Wilberta said.
"I'm sorry I'm such a crabapple today.
We've been inside too long.
Let's go out."
Buckley smiled a wide smile
and jumped to his feet.
"Last one out is a *rotten* apple!"

SHOVELING OUT

Buckley unlatched his front door.
It wouldn't open!
He pulled harder.
Oooooffff!
Snow had drifted
almost to the top!

"I'll have to shovel out.," he said.

"How will you do that?" Wilberta asked.

"I'll climb out the window
and dig a path to the door."

"Good idea," Wilberta said.

Buckley got his snow shovel
from the front closet.

Buckley pushed open the window.
"Careful," said Wilberta.
"It looks slippery!"

"Whoooppps!" Buckley cried.
"Buckley!" Wilberta shouted.

"Oh, Buckley!
Are you okay?"

"Guess I don't need the shovel,"
Buckley said.
Wilberta laughed.
"Now that's *quiet* rolling.
Not even a *hup hup!*"

A GOOD TEAM

"Let's make a snowrabbit,"
Buckley said.
"Let's make it look like
one of my cousins," said Wilberta.
They began to roll up
a ball of snow,
and pat it smooth.
Buckley sang a hedgehog song
while they worked.

   "Roly-poly-oly-oh
   Sings a hedgehog in the snow
   When you see him say 'hello'
   He'll wave and call back 'oly-oh!' "

"It's going to be
a great snowrabbit," Buckley said.
"But I can't reach any higher.
You'll have to finish it, Wilberta."
"You could make the head,"
suggested Wilberta.
Buckley smiled. "Great idea."
He rolled up a ball of snow,
and patted it into
the shape of a rabbit head.

Then he hurried into his house.
He came back with
some nuts,
two corn husks,
and an old vest.
He pushed the chestnuts
into the snow head
to make eyes and a nose.
Then he poked the corn husks
into the top for ears.
"There," he called to Wilberta.
"Will you lift it up for me?"

Wilberta set the head
on top of the snowrabbit.
"Wonderful!" she said.
"It does look like
one of my cousins.
It even has our
family's floppy ear."

"Wait," Buckley said.
"One more thing."
He ran back in the house
and brought out his broom.

He pulled four straws
out of the broom.
"This cousin needs whiskers," he said.
Wilberta stuck the straws
on either side
of the snowrabbit's nose,
then added two carrots.
They both stood back
to admire their work.
"It looks good," Buckley said.
"I like it when we do things together."
"Me, too," Wilberta agreed.
"We make a good team."
"Do you suppose
a good team deserves
some cake?" Buckley asked.
Wilberta laughed.
"Yes I do," she said.
"Let's eat some right now!"

STORM CLOUDS

After most of the snow melted
Wilberta went home
to open up her house
and plant her garden.

As the days grew warmer
clouds sometimes formed.
Buckley watched them carefully.
If they turned dark
he hurried home.
When thunder rolled
through the sky
he rolled under his bed.

One sunny morning
Wilberta came to Buckley's house
carrying her picnic basket.
"I baked carrot muffins," she said.
"And I made chestnut butter
sandwiches.
Let's go for a picnic."
"Great idea!" Buckley said.
"I'll bring some mint tea."
They hiked through the woods
and ate lunch.
After lunch they
picked wild strawberries.
Buckley didn't notice
the sky growing dark.
Then he heard
a rumble of thunder.

He dropped his berries
and started to run.
"I have to go home now," he called.
"Buckley!" Wilberta shouted.
"Wait!"
"What's the matter?"
But Buckley was almost out of sight.
Wilberta hurried after him.
When she got to Buckley's house
big raindrops were falling
She knocked and knocked.
Buckley didn't answer.
She opened the door. "Buckley?"
Still no answer.
She thought she heard
a muffled voice
coming from the bedroom.

"Buckley, where are you?"
Wilberta called.

"Unner ah beh."

Wilberta went into the bedroom.

"What are you doing under there?"
she asked.

"Waiting," Buckley said.

"Waiting for what?"

"For the thunder to be over."

"Oh," Wilberta said.

She thought a minute.

"Well, thunder isn't anything
to be afraid of."

"I'm not afraid." Buckley said.

"Oh," said Wilberta.

She went to Buckley's front closet
and looked through his winter things.

In a minute Wilberta
came back to the bedroom.
"Just in case
you ever are afraid," she said,
"put these earmuffs on when
you see dark clouds."
Buckley rolled out from
under the bed.
"Great idea!" he said.
"Glad to help," Wilberta said.
"What did you say?" asked Buckley.
Wilberta just smiled.

LUCKY FRIENDS

It was the wettest spring
Buckley could remember.
The stream was running fast
into Perkin's dam.
Buckley shook his head.
"Wilberta's house is
very close to the stream,"
he said to Perkins.
"You are right about that,"
said Perkins.

"I'm going there now," Buckley said.
He tried not to worry.
He sang a hedgehog song.

"Roly-poly-oly-ain
Sings a hedgehog in the rain
As he passes down the lane
He'll wave and call out 'oly-ain!' "

"You are too close to the stream,"
Buckley said to Wilberta.
"Why don't you move
up the hill to my house
until the spring rains are over?"
"You worry too much,"
Wilberta said.
"I'm fine right here."

When Buckley went to bed
it was raining again.
Sometime in the dark night
something went THUMP.
He jumped out of bed
and lit his lantern.
He opened the front door.
The wind whipped a tree branch
against his house.
WHUMP.
Water rushed past his door,
down the path
toward the stream.

Buckley thought of Wilberta.
Was she all right?
He had to find out.
He splashed down the path
holding the lantern high.
He tripped on a tree root
and dropped the lantern.
He scrambled up
and grabbed it.
It sputtered and flickered.

Lightning streaked the sky.
Thunder rumbled
through the darkness.
Buckley held tight to the lantern.
He was soaked
and shivering cold.
It had never seemed so far
to Wilberta's house.

At last, he saw her front door.
Water swirled all around it.
He waded to Wilberta's
bedroom window.
He tapped hard.
"Wilberta!
Wilberta! Wake up!"
Wilberta's face appeared.
She unlatched the window.
"Buckley!
There's water in my bedroom!
It's deep!"

"Hurry!" Buckley shouted.
"Come to my house!"
Wilberta nodded and disappeared.
Buckley waded to the door.
He tugged it open.
Out came Wilberta
with a rush of water!
Buckley grabbed her by the paw.

They sloshed up
the path together.
Lightning flashed.
Thunder echoed
through the woods.
Water was still running past
Buckley's house,
but it was dry inside.
Buckley built a fire.
"Lucky I'm uphill
from the stream," he said.
"Lucky for me," said Wilberta.
She warmed her back.

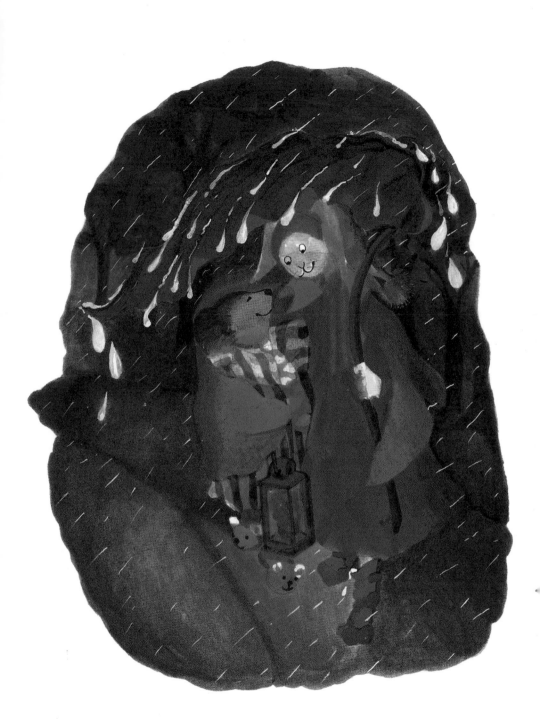

Buckley carried in
two cups of tea.
"You were right to worry, Buckley,"
said Wilberta.
I should have listened to you."
"You were right, too, Wilberta,"
Buckley said.
"I was?"
"Yes, you were.
I didn't even wear
my earmuffs tonight.
Thunder *is* nothing to be afraid of."
"Then we're both lucky
and we're both right!" Wilberta said.